I AM PLAYING

BY MERCER MAYER

Random House 🏠 New York

Library of Congress Catalog Card Number: 94-68289   ISBN 0-679-87350-3
Manufactured in Italy   10 9 8 7 6 5 4 3 2 1

🐸 GREEN FROG PUBLISHERS, INC. / J. R. SANSEVERE BOOK

I like to play.
I play with my puppy.

I play with my friends.

We play with my kite.

We play on my swing set.

I play all day long.
Then I am very tired.

I play with my animals.

I play with my puzzles.

I play in the bathtub.

We play school.

We play with her jack-in-the-box.

We play with my camera.

We play with her kitchen set.

I play with my sister.

We play in the mud.

We play kickball.

We play space invaders.

We play pirates.